This
book
belongs to:
....

TEN IN A HURRY

LO COLE

sourcebooks
jabberwocky

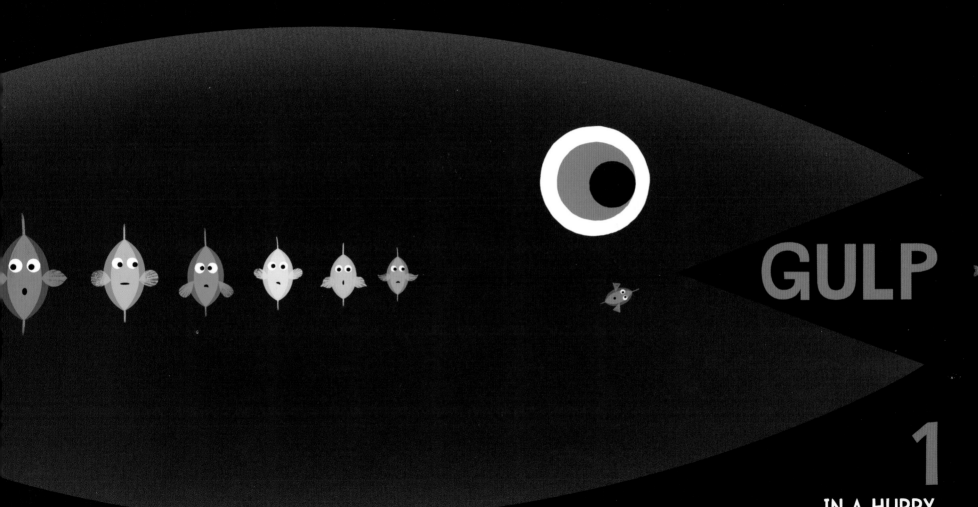

BROWN GETS SWALLOWED,
THERE'S ONLY ONE LEFT.

GULP

1

IN A HURRY,
RED AND UNBEATEN.

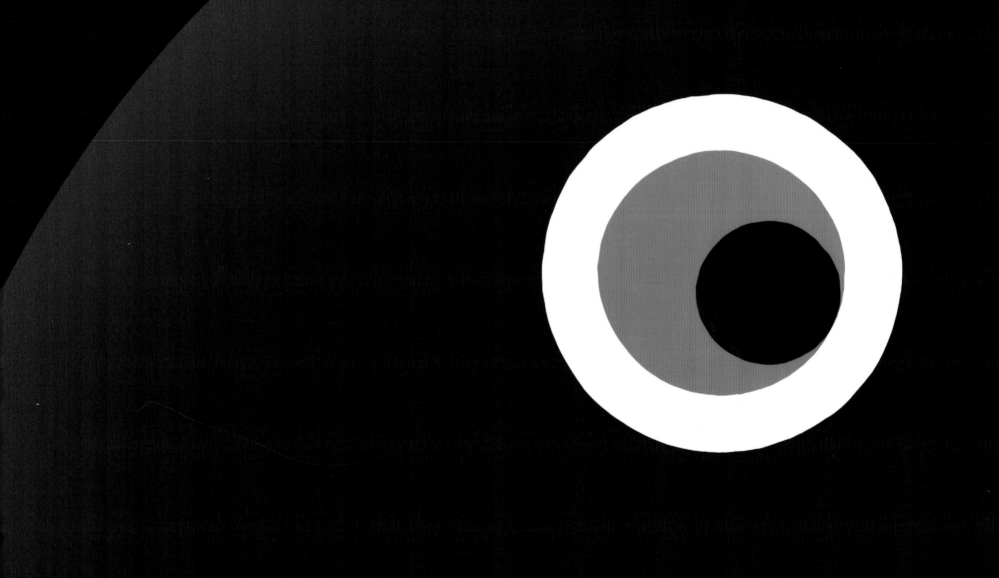

OFF GOES ORANGE.
THAT LEAVES TWO.

GULP

2
IN A HURRY,
WHO COULD HAVE GUESSED?

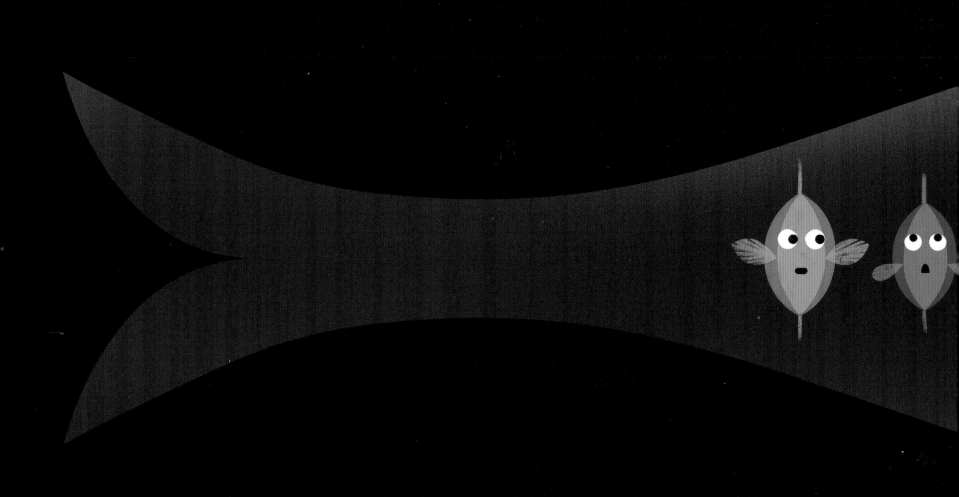

GULP

3

IN A HURRY,

"WE WON'T BE EATEN!"

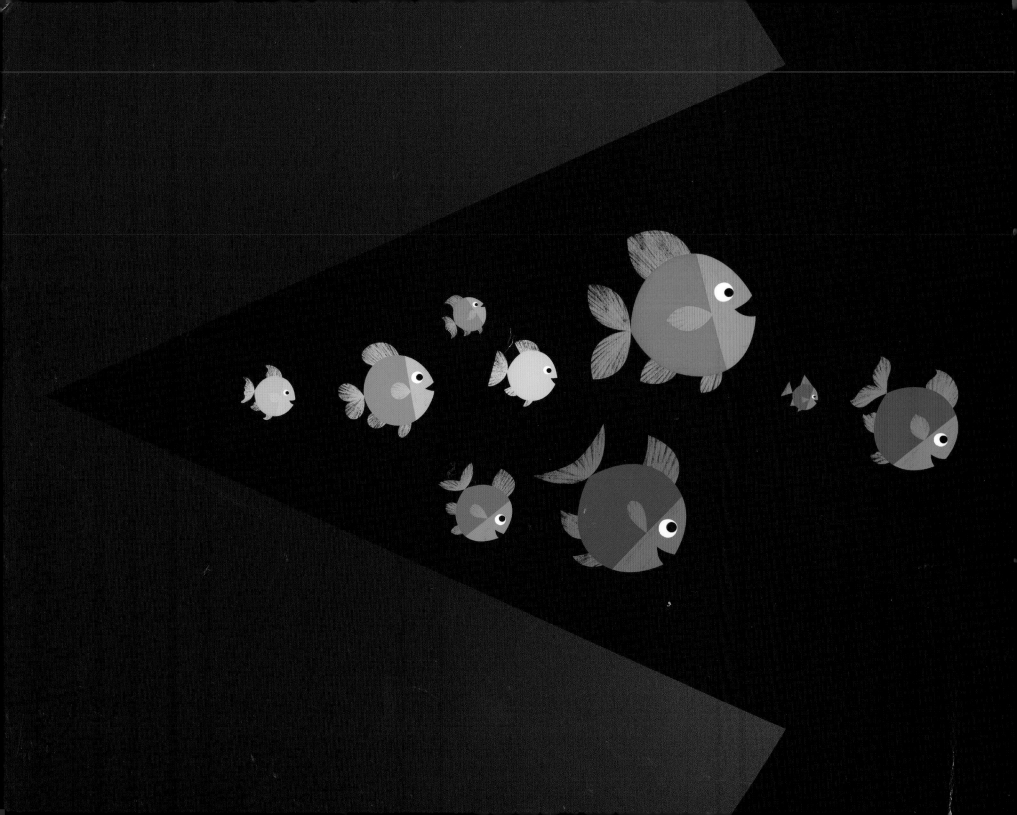

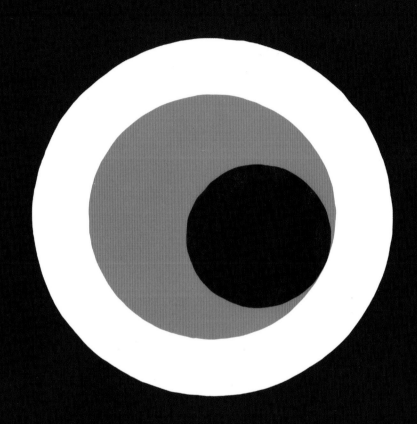

YELLS OUT LOUD...

9

IN A BELLY TOTALLY AGREE.
WITH ONE MIGHTY

BURP

THEY ALL BURST FREE!

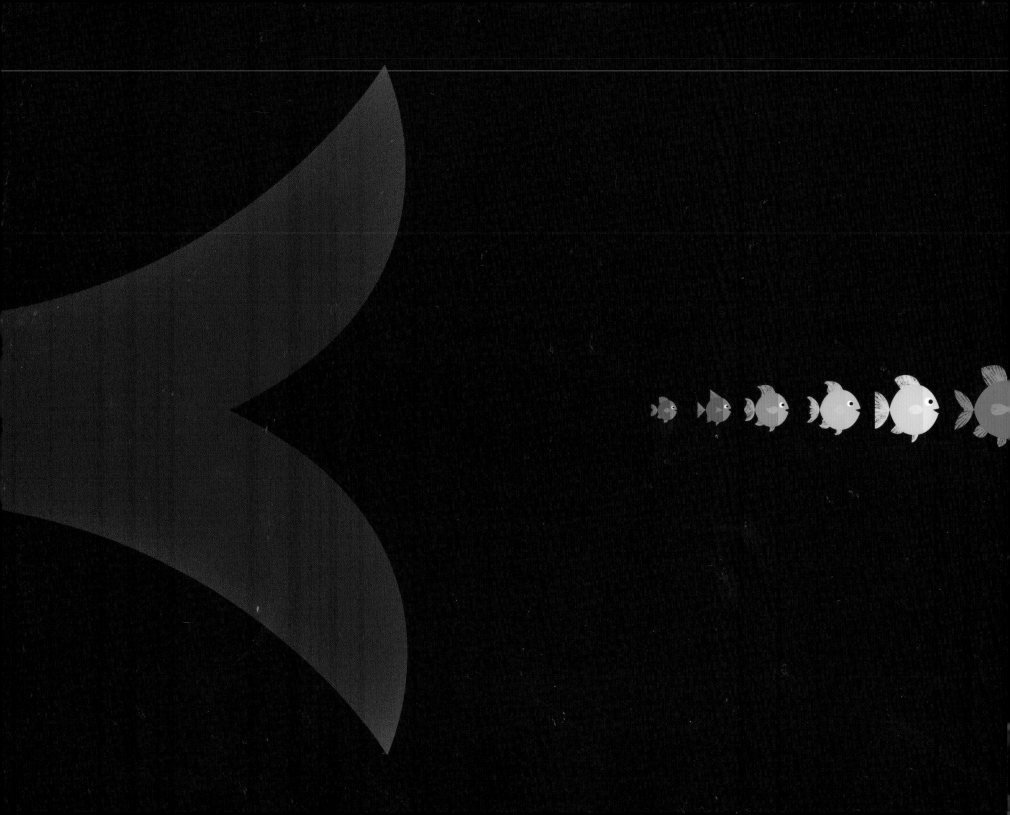

10
IN A HURRY,
SWIMMING IN A LINE.
THEY BETTER GET A MOVE ON
TO GET TO SCHOOL ON TIME!

Published by Sourcebooks Jabberwocky, an imprint of Sourcebooks Kids
P.O. Box 4410, Naperville, Illinois 60567–4410
(630) 961-3900
SOURCEBOOKSKIDS.COM

Library of Congress Cataloging-in-Publication Data is on file with the publisher.

Source of Production: 1010 Printing Asia Limited, North Point, Hong Kong, China
Date of Production: June 2021
Run Number: 5021728
Printed and bound in China.
OGP 10 9 8 7 6 5 4 3 2 1